SHADOWS

SLEEPING DRAGONS BOOK 4

OPHELIA BELL

Shadows
Copyright © 2014 Ophelia Bell
Cover Art Designed by Dawné Dominique
Photograph Copyrights © Fotolio.com, DepositPhotos.com, CanStock.com

All rights reserved. No part of this book may be reproduced in any form or by any electronic means, including information storage and retrieval systems, without permission in writing from the author, except by a reviewer who may quote brief passages in review.

This is a work of fiction. Names, places, characters, and events are fictitious in every regard. Any similarities to actual events and persons, living or dead, is purely coincidental. Any trademarks, service marks, product names, or named features are assumed to be the property of their respective owners, and are used only for reference. There is no implied endorsement if any of these terms are used.

Published by Ophelia Bell
UNITED STATES

ISBN-13: 978-1544293202
ISBN-10: 1544293208

ALSO BY OPHELIA BELL

SLEEPING DRAGONS SERIES

Animus
Tabula Rasa
Gemini
Shadows
Nexus
Ascend

RISING DRAGONS SERIES

Night Fire
Breath of Destiny
Breath of Memory
Breath of Innocence
Breath of Desire
Breath of Love
Breath of Flame & Shadow
Breath of Fate
Sisters of Flame

IMMORTAL DRAGONS SERIES

Dragon Betrayed
Dragon Blues
Dragon Void

STANDALONE EROTIC TALES

After You
Out of the Cold

OPHELIA BELL TABOO

Burying His Desires

•

Blackmailing Benjamin
Betraying Benjamin
Belonging to Benjamin

•

Casey's Secrets
Casey's Discovery
Casey's Surrender

Even love has a dark side.

CHAPTER ONE

Darkness was a perpetual irritation, particularly for a creature like Kol. He was not only trapped in it, he was a part of it. For centuries he'd lived without light. The darkness of the temple he lived in was incidental compared to the inky black of the mood he'd wallowed in since the day the exit doors had slid closed, trapping him and his multitude of brethren inside to sleep for half a millennium.

He'd lost count of the days since the light had gone out, but guessed it had to be close to the five centuries the dragons' cycle of sleep should last. He could have done the math but didn't care to. What purpose would it serve to mark time in such a place? Particularly when you were the only one awake.

That wasn't precisely true. They could all be conscious if they chose to be, but aside from himself and the Guardians, the others had a choice in their static jade forms to sleep through the centuries. For the first week he'd heard the others in his mind, speaking in subdued voices. Gradually the voices had grown fewer and fewer as they'd succumbed to sleep, until only his twin siblings had been awake, trying to bolster his mood as always. *We love you, Kol. We know it's an honor to be chosen for your job. We'd do it in a heartbeat.*

Finishing each other's sentences, Aurin and Aurik were as oblivious to Kol's demons as they were to their own strange and shifting symmetry. The two of them reminded him of a gyroscope. As long as their balance of power exchange remained, he believed the Earth probably still maintained its axis. If Aurin and Aurik ever faltered, then Kol would worry about the fate of dragonkind.

In spite of their sentiments, they never would have been chosen for his job. The job of Shadow was only for a black dragon like him. Brilliant gold as the twins were, they were better suited for uplifting humanity than skulking around in the dark.

Skulking was something he was good at, and had been even before doing it for five hundred years. Technically, he *was* asleep. At least his body was. But his magic, unique to black dragons, allowed him to manifest through his breath. While his physical body slept on, frozen in black jade, the shadow of his breath coalesced into a smaller, human form and lurked about the temple like a ghost, ensuring the security of all who slept within.

Tedious, monotonous, dreary, boring—he could think of so many other terms to describe his job. Dragon law dictated that a Shadow watch over the brood each cycle, and he'd been chosen for this one. Though he was not precisely *chosen* so much as compelled. True, he was probably the best candidate for the position, but traditionally potential Shadows were given a choice because of the psychological strain it took. He was the first one who'd been compelled to do it as a penalty for poor behavior.

He chuckled to himself at that. Speak out against the council's outdated ideals and get shoved in a dark prison. Granted, he'd have been here anyway, but at least he could have slept through the whole ordeal and let one of the others like him do the job.

He'd undeniably broken the rules, as archaic as they were. *Willfully* broken the rules, the council had said when he stood before them on the eve of his sentence. As if the heart knew anything beyond what made it beat.

Generations had passed since. The lover he'd accepted the sentence for was long dead, but the certainty didn't help quell the excitement that welled in him knowing how close they were to the end of their confinement. What would he find on the outside? Dragon lore only spoke of vast changes in each cycle, but they were an infinitely adaptable race. Would he look for her? Her descendants? He suddenly wished fervently that he'd had the foresight to mate with her before they'd been parted. He'd already broken one rule by falling in love with her, why not one more by getting her with child? Oh, would *that* have left the council in a bind considering the child wouldn't have been born until after the temple was sealed. But he hadn't left anything behind but regret and a now dead lover.

It happened sometimes. Young dragons breaking the rules prior to their slumber. The marked mates often died of sorrow if the dragon had no elder family to take them in. Any children of such a union would be taken and raised by the council, but would grow up nameless, forbidden from acquiring treasure. They would spend their lives in service to the council and tended to die young, only living out roughly half of a dragon's multiple-century life span. Slavery and grief were the last things

Kol wanted for a mate and child of his own. His lover may have grieved him, but at least he'd left her with the freedom to move on.

Eveline.

Even thinking the name after the centuries without her brought back the memories of their time together. The loss twisted painfully in his chest, as sharp as a blade. The discomfort was enough to make him pause in his mindless patrol of the temple corridors. Sleep would be nice right now. Sleep would have been nice for the last five hundred years, but it wasn't for him. And he didn't want to be the one who slept on the job, even if it were a possibility. Hah.

At least he had the Guardians for company during his daily patrols. They were the second defense if their temple were ever prematurely breached, so they existed in a more aroused state of wakefulness than the rest. Kol chuckled at *that* thought. *All* of them were asleep in an *aroused* state, even his massive slumbering form in the room beside the Queen's sported its own huge erection. They had to be ready when the awakening ritual began. The Guardians were just the most visible. He often wondered what they would look like if the temple were ever actually attacked and they were forced into action. White dragons with massive erections might distract even the most determined grave robber.

The thought made him laugh.

"How goes it, Roka?" he asked, pausing on his rounds in front of his closest friend of the Guardians.

"You tease me with your voice, Shadow. If I had breath, we could have a proper duel and see who triumphed." The voice permeated Kol's

mind rather than the air between him and the rigid white statue he stood before. Kol still reached out a hand and rested it on Roka's shoulder.

Kol laughed. "If you had breath you know mine would overtake yours in a second."

"We'll see who gathers the most treasure when we awaken. I'll wager I get more, even as a guardian."

"I'll wager you do, too, friend. I don't see the allure in treasure. Not even humans, as pretty and vibrant as they are."

"You deserve more after this cycle. You deserve concubines."

"I do, do I? You know that the Court is already entitled to a multitude of partners if we choose, right?"

Kol smirked at the silence his friend responded with.

"Then why don't you seem happy about that prospect?"

Mother of all...Roka did always ask the most irritating questions.

"I just want one woman. One sweet morsel to savor for the next few decades after this temple is finally opened. Someone whose world I can change enough to see in her eyes how much I mean to her and her alone."

"But you're not a collector? It's our nature. I want at least two. At least I know what I would do with two. More than that might be...complicated."

Kol laughed. "Yes, more than two becomes problematic. All I want to collect is the touch of her skin, the silky dew between her thighs, the little sounds she makes that lets me know my touch is affecting her."

He wandered away from the conversation with his fingertips tingling as though they'd already touched hot skin, memories of Eveline playing over and over in his mind.

CHAPTER TWO

The sweet dark of sleep was a hard commodity to retain. Hallie questioned her own sanity every morning when the camp awakened and she was forced to rise with the rest. She wasn't a morning person, but apparently she was outnumbered. And since she was trying her best to conform to the ideals of the expeditionary type, she rose, too. Or she tried to, anyway.

It was still fucking dark in their jungle camp, but the entire group had been edgy all night knowing the next leg of their trek would likely take them to their final destination.

She opened her eyes and glared at the edge of her sleeping bag, resisting rising for just a few more moments. Five minutes… she could squeeze in five more minutes of sleep if she tried really hard. She clenched her eyes shut, trying to bring back the delicious dream she'd been having about Kris. In the dream he'd had a massive erection and was about to shove it in her.

Something tickled her cheek and she swept her palm over it. The tickle came back a second later, an irritating distraction from her hopeful dreams. She smacked her hand on her cheek smartly, wishing whatever it was would go away.

The tickle returned, accompanied by a throaty giggle.

"Camille, you're in for it," she murmured gruffly against her sleeping bag.

A hard sigh sounded behind her. "I'm sorry. You said you wanted help waking up, so I thought I'd try this. It was fun until you started sounding bitchy."

"Don't take it personally. I'm always bitchy at this time of day. At least if I'm awake."

She rolled over and smiled sleepily at her blonde friend.

"Did he take the bait?" she asked.

Camille scowled. "No. I messed it up. He just…" She flushed brightly and bit her lower lip hard enough to make it shine bright red. Her discomfort made Hallie reach out to comfort her.

"Sweetie, don't do that…Eben loves you, I know it."

Camille looked like she was about to cry. "So why…?" Her lip quivered before she could get another word out.

"Just focus on work for now, alright? He'll come around, I promise."

She felt like a fraud spouting useless advice to the girl. Camille was brilliant and beautiful, in a weirdly delicate way, but completely ill-equipped to deal with a crush on a guy. At least Hallie hadn't been lying about Eben's feelings. That was one detail she'd bet her life on if she had to, considering how she'd seen Eben watching Camille every day since the expedition had begun. He'd cast furtive glances at the pretty linguist, then look away and spend the next hour or so with a broody crease between his eyebrows. Hallie wasn't the least bit surprised, either. Camille possessed the perfect combination of sensuality and innocence that could drive men mad. At least one man.

Hallie felt like a fraud in a lot of other ways, too. Mostly because she *was* a fraud. She didn't know archeology from a hole in the wall, yet she'd convinced Erika somehow that she belonged with them. It wasn't as if she'd been dead weight during their expedition, at least. If anything she'd been more valuable than the others during the rugged trek. It helped growing up in the wilderness of Canada. Tropical hazards were different, but her constitution could handle them.

And they were very far away from the bullshit she'd left behind, which was the biggest plus. No one would even think to look for her here, least of all the asshole she'd conceived this entire crazy plan to escape. Still, every day the easy camaraderie of the others left her feeling like an outsider. She'd lied to join them and kept lying to cover up her lack of experience. She'd only done the bare minimum of research prior to applying for the assistantship required to join the expedition. She'd learned how to manipulate potential bosses years ago. Be pretty and clean, drop all the right words, show the right level of confidence. Her past few jobs were acquired under the same pretense, which was a requirement when you had things to hide.

This one had been a little different. She'd only had two days to set it up. Posing as an esoteric scholar should have been easy but it had proven to be the most stressful interview of her life. Ultimately she'd given up on the exhaustive planning she usually employed and just threw on jeans and a t-shirt, studied her notes on the subject in question, and headed out the door. She was likely dead either way it went, so why stress over details?

Somehow, it had worked.

Erika hadn't even glanced at Hallie's fabricated curriculum vitae. She'd met Hallie in a tiny cafe west of campus. They'd exchanged pleasantries, then Erika had completely ignored the folder of papers she had in front of her and proceeded to grill Hallie on her personal history.

It had been a shock, but Hallie had answered honestly, at least until Erika got to the college questions. The best lies always held a kernel of truth. In the end, the woman she sold to Erika was an intelligent girl restricted by her upbringing and rising up from nothing. It wasn't very far from the truth. She'd always wanted to be that woman, but poor decisions had gotten in her way.

When their interview concluded, Erika had stuck out her hand and pulled her into a tight hug. Flabbergasted at the quick acceptance, Hallie had hugged back. She nodded and murmured a thank you when Erika expressed how she couldn't wait to see her the next day when their flight to Indonesia departed.

CHAPTER THREE

Kol's skin itched. He would give anything to be free of his stone prison and able to stretch his corporeal limbs. To dive into the pool that occupied the center of his chamber and soak in the warmth of the water, wash away five hundred years of regret that he hadn't done more to keep the woman he loved. Eveline's face had faded from his memory. All he had left were fragments of her that came to him in dreams—the softness of her skin, the heat of her breath, the earthy scent of her sex.

Perhaps Roka was right. Maybe he should have avoided focusing so intently on one human. Most dragons avoided favoritism among their treasure, choosing instead to distribute their attention evenly among many humans. There were no limits, according to dragon law. Dragons could possess as much treasure as they were capable of attracting to themselves. His distant predecessors had boasted throngs of loyal subjects, but over the generations, dragons had gradually grown more focused, choosing to reserve their attention for a few very loyal humans. He was the first one who had ever balked at tradition so much that he'd chosen one woman outside his parents' collection, which had been his first mistake.

Young dragons were often encouraged to appreciate their family's treasures, but Kol's tastes were not quite what his parents or the council would have liked him to have. The twins were the same. He supposed it wasn't so much the singularity of his choice that caused the council to punish him, but that he'd never marked her. But how did you mar such a beautiful, perfect creature as she was?

The idea of humans like Eveline as mere possessions left a bad taste in his mouth. When the doors to the temple opened he would be expected yet again to collect treasure. He was under no delusions what that really meant. Humans were status symbols to dragons. The more he possessed, the more respect he received. It didn't help that the urge was innate. He had *wanted* to mark Eveline so many times, yet rejected his own nature in exchange for knowing she was with him of her own volition. Until the council had found out and destroyed his perfect life.

Loving her wasn't the crime. Showing her his nature yet leaving her unmarked was. The magic of the mark made humans intensely loyal and incapable of betrayal. But to Kol there was far more power in gaining the trust and loyalty of a human without resorting to magic.

So they'd forced him to do nothing *but* resort to magic for the last five hundred years. Manifesting his human form with his breath on a daily basis still hadn't changed his opinion on marking humans, but it had made him appreciate the magic he was capable of more than he had before. Not quite solid, without considerable focus and effort his breath could still affect his environment in subtle ways. He could open doors with it, but most often merely wisped between the cracks. He could sense the smooth texture of the walls that held him in, the cool jade tiles of the floor beneath his shadowy tread. He couldn't dive into the water of his pool, but he could cast ripples across its surface.

And when the surface doors finally opened, he could sense the change in pressure causing every molecule of his breath to vibrate, the sensation transferring instantaneously to his true form, frozen in jade. For the first time in half a millennium, his perpetually erect cock throbbed in anticipation.

He sent his shadow to the surface where he lingered in the darkness, watching the seven humans trickle in, each one marveling at the interior of the temple as they began to explore it.

He watched their leader intently at first. She wasn't the most beautiful of the women, but she exuded power he had rarely encountered in human women. This century might prove very interesting if other women were like her. She easily subjugated the male who followed close behind her, and he didn't seem the least bit put down by her dismissiveness. He only had eyes for the prettiest female among them—a petite and round-bottomed blonde. A tasty morsel by any stretch. The man had good taste.

The others followed down the long staircase, oblivious to his presence blended into the shadows. The third woman's scent reached him before he saw her, tickling at his nostrils like the soft down of aromatic feathers. Sweet and pungent, like the scent of the earth right after a rainstorm. With cautious steps, she came down the staircase, brushing past him so closely he could feel her heat and sense the rising arousal that the magic of the temple incited in all the humans who entered it.

The familiar and unwelcome instinct to possess rose so suddenly it made him dizzy. He moved behind her and leaned closer, reaching one ethereal hand up to trace the line of her neck. Skin still damp from the heat of the jungle met his touch. He let his eyes follow the path of his fingers down to her shoulder blade, then across to the front, chasing the path of a tiny bead of sweat as it traveled along the crest of her collarbone.

He stood behind her looking down at that tiny droplet of moisture, poised in the arc of bone and skin that pointed down between her breasts. His ghostly fingertip still rested at the edge of it, the rest of his hand splayed to avoid touching her skin, though he would love to feel the warmth of her against his palm.

Overcome by a sudden thirst, he licked his lips. The droplet quivered then skidded across tanned skin and pores, lower, lower, Kol's eyes following it all the way. What he wouldn't give to be that orb of wetness traveling between her breasts, only to be absorbed at the end of the journey. Or perhaps lapped up by some lucky man. One of the other travelers maybe?

He inhaled deeply, hoping to impress the aroma of her into his memory alongside the scent of the only other woman he'd ever thought he'd want. He couldn't deny the pull from this one, though.

Some force against Kol's back caused his his shadowy form to dissipate like a warm, insistent breeze diluting a bank of fog. He reformed to the side of the stairway and glared at the large, male figure who followed the young woman. Dark eyes stared straight back at him with unmistakable recognition.

"You can see me?" Kol asked, sending the thought out with intent to the man. The man didn't reply but only nodded quickly. He shifted his attention to the woman when she turned in response to his proximity.

"What is it, Kris?" she asked.

"Thought I saw a bug, but it's gone now," he said with a twitch of his lips. "Must've caught a ride from outside."

"Ugh, I'll be done with bugs after this trip. You don't think there are any inside, do you?"

The man named Kris chuckled. "Not sealed up the way this place is. Legend says that dragons tended to repel most other living things, including insects. Humans tend to be more like moths to a flame for them, though." He darted his eyes pointedly in the direction of Kol's shadow.

"Who's the moth and who's the flame?" Kol heard in a pointed tone in his mind.

"You really believe this stuff, don't you?" she asked.

"I believe it because it's the truth," Kris said matter-of-factly.

"I know, I know. Your *destiny* was to guide us here. Erika's bought into it, too. Me…I'll believe it when I see it, I guess."

The man's identity became clear to Kol with those words, and the effect Kris had on Kol's incorporeal form made more sense. This group was without a doubt the chosen few who would awaken them. It really was finally happening. Today would be his last day trapped here.

"You're the Catalyst, aren't you?" Kol asked. He moved back to walk beside Kris, now more conscious of the barrier of magic that cocooned the man, preventing Kol from moving closer. He

kept his eyes on the back of the woman's neck as they walked, watching yet another bead of sweat trace her skin and wishing he could follow its path, dart his long forked tongue out to taste it.

"Yes. But you're the Shadow. Didn't expect to be greeted at the door like this. It's an honor." The man's thoughts reverberated in Kol's mind. He had the blood, too. Otherwise he'd never have been able to communicate that way.

"I'm more than ready to get the ritual started. One more day and we'll all be free, thanks to the seven of you."

"I'll have them itching to get going after supper tonight. Trust me, friend, I'm as ready as you are." Kris reached between his thighs, adjusting himself in emphasis.

"I don't envy you the waiting, but I understand. It's been five centuries since I last touched a woman. Please tell me what that one's name is. I have to mark her."

Kris laughed. *"I've heard of you. The accounts of your little rebellion are a cautionary tale at the monastery where I was raised. Refused to properly mark your lover after showing her what you were. I believed in your argument, when I learned of it. Now you talk like your principles have changed. Did the punishment sink in?"*

"No, but it's the only way to complete the ritual. If they're going to force it on me, I must be sure she's willing when I have to do it."

"That may be tricky. She's a bit of a rebel, too. Her name is Hallie, but she isn't who she pretends to be. Good luck to you."

Kol kept to the shadows for the rest of the evening, but never let his eyes wander too far from Hallie. Watching the magic's gradual effect on her kept him enthralled. She savored the dinner Kris cooked them like it was a sensuous treat, eyes closed with every bite, tongue darting out to lick her full lips and make sure she didn't miss a single shred of flavor. Kol could smell the dragon magic that infused the meal from the fresh temple water Kris had used to cook it.

Kris did his job well after the meal was over, encouraging their leader and her human lover to begin the ritual and nudging the others in the right direction when the time came. The man was subtle, but effective. The first couple went willingly, followed shortly by the pretty blonde with the plump bottom. The others stayed in their camp and tried to sleep for a few hours, but the heightened excitement left them tossing and turning, except for Hallie who seemed to sleep soundly.

Then the young Greek man with the deep sadness left, along with the most skeptical member of the group—a man they called Corey, who seemed to grow angrier the more aroused he became.

That left Hallie, curled up in her bedroll in a shadowy alcove away from the glowing fire pit. Kol only watched at first, his mind drifting to memories of the last time he'd been with Eveline. His old lover had awakened one morning and found him watching her, much like he watched Hallie now.

"You have the look of a very patient cat waiting for the chase," Eveline had said. "You could have had me in your jaws a hundred times while I slept, helpless."

"I prefer knowing that you're choosing not to run when I decide to take you." He slipped down beside her warm curves, cupped one breast and pressed lips and tongue to the juncture at her neck and shoulder.

She nestled back against him and tilted her head to grant better access to her skin. "I would never run from you. Not even in my dreams. I was dreaming of you just like this, you know."

"Hmm, like this?" he asked, moving one hand lower and teasing the downy thicket between her thighs. Dewy wetness clung to her fringe. He slid his fingertips a little deeper into the heat of her, enjoying the soft sigh she emitted when he found her swollen bud already slick with her juices.

"Yes. Just once I'd like to wake up to you already inside me. To believe we'd never been parted even during sleep."

Pleasing Eveline had always been paramount, but he'd never gotten the opportunity to fulfill her request. The council had learned of his misbehavior and had sent him immediately to the temple. He hadn't even been allowed to see Eveline one last time.

This could be his chance for redemption. To do things differently. But the ritual was already underway and the one he believed he was meant for was here sleeping.

Hallie rolled onto her side and kicked her covers off, displaying long, tanned legs that led up to the curve of wide hips hugged by dark fabric. She seemed to have an affinity for black. Most of the garments he'd watched her strip off earlier had been varying shades of black. She hadn't been modest around her teammates, either. The only one with a shred of modesty had been the pretty blonde, and the only overtly sexual interaction among the group had been between the leader and her lover.

It must be a very different world for men and women to be so uninhibited with each other. The other men had looked at Hallie appreciatively, but with a surprising level of respect. Dragons looked at each other the same way, but in his experience, human men rarely treated human women like equals.

Now Hallie lay nearly naked aside from her small, black undergarments. The sleeveless top she wore had ridden up to expose her belly. Her thighs shifted against each other, sending a hint of her arousal to him.

Sweet Mother, he needed to touch her again. He needed her to wake up and come to him soon. To open his chamber and awaken his body so he could mark her and complete his phase of the ritual. *No*, he thought. *So she can learn the truth and make the choice. I refuse to do it unless she is willing. Damn the others.* But he knew he owed it to his brethren to try. His disagreement had been with the Council, not the other dragons trapped in the temple with him. So he would try. And the first step was to plan his silent seduction while she slept.

CHAPTER FOUR

The whisper of her lover's breath had always been enough to send Hallie into fits of desire. She responded especially well, when still fuzzy and languid from sleep, to the light touch of him caressing her skin, tracing the curve of her body from shoulder to hip and down over her thigh, while his hot breath tickled the back of her neck.

A soft sigh escaped her lips as those very sensations roused her just enough for her body to respond, yet not quite awakening her fully. A large, warm hand slipped beneath the fabric of her tank top and fingertips teased at the underside of one breast, barely grazing the edge of her nipple.

"Yes," she whispered, pressing back against his hot arousal by reflex.

A deep, appreciative rumble vibrated against her back. His lips grazed the nape of her neck, sending a vivid tingle down her spine and between her legs.

His light caresses continued, slipping down her stomach, past her navel and beneath the waistband of her panties. Her hips twitched at the slide of gentle, probing fingertips exploring between the eager folds of her pussy. She moaned and quivered, pressing harder back against his rigid, naked length.

He gripped the crotch of her panties and tugged them hard to the side. She cried out with harsh joy when he pressed two fingers into her, then slid them out again. He teased her with a few soft strokes against her throbbing clit before he plunged his fingers deep into her wet cunt.

The dreamlike state Hallie had been in during the whole experience began to fall away with each deep plunge of his fingers into her needy pussy, her ecstasy so pure and present it could only be real and not a figment of her unconscious mind.

Confusion gripped her, wrenching her stomach into a quick, tight knot. Her eyes flew open. But what she thought was a dream didn't dissipate, nor did the pleasure of it, in spite of her mild panic.

In the span of a second her mind and body warred with each other, the urge to fling herself away from the unexpected attention at odds with the incredible, mind-blowing pleasure of it. Her desire won out and she surrendered, closing her eyes and pushing back against him with more fervent thrusts of her own, clenching her muscles tighter around the heavy weight of the fingers plunging into her.

It could be any of the four men, she thought. And would she care if it were? But Jesus Fucking Christ, whoever it was, he was giving her the best finger fuck of her life.

His lips pressed against her shoulder, grazing up along the curve of her neck until they brushed against her ear. Hot breath gusted out, carrying with it a word she didn't understand.

Is it Kris? It must be Kris.

She had heard Kris speak in Thai a few times, and remembered the look he'd given her when he picked up her empty bowl after dinner. The thought made her smile in delight. She was sure he'd followed Erika to have a quick tryst in one of the dragon temple's dark corridors, but clearly he'd come back frustrated enough to crawl into her sleeping bag and have his way with her. It was even better than the fantasy she'd had of him during dinner. It made her even more eager to fuck him back as enthusiastically as she could.

Not even caring if she might wake the others, she cried out, "Oh, yes! Fuck me. Make me come!"

The fingertips between her thighs rubbed in even more delicious tormenting circles against her clit. God, she was close.

He murmured something else in her ear she didn't understand, but if she didn't know better the tone of his voice seemed to hold regret. Then without another sound or breath, the sensations dissipated entirely, leaving her abruptly untouched and frustrated as hell with a sopping wet and aching pussy.

She rolled over and yelled out. "Hey! Where the fuck did you go? Come back! You asshole, I wasn't even…I was so *close!*"

The sound of a thump and a curse carried across from the other side of the campsite and she twisted back around to see where it had come from.

"Corey?"

"Yeah, sorry. I…uh…didn't mean to bother you." He glanced at her and quickly averted his eyes, resuming whatever work he was doing.

She blinked at him in surprise, completely and utterly confused by his presence now. He was fully clothed. Maybe a little flushed but mostly he looked irritated. There was no way it could've been him.

"Did you see Kris just now?" she asked.

Without looking at her he nodded. "A little bit ago, back in the corridor behind the throne. He's still there as far as I know. Why?"

"No, right here…ah…*with me* I mean. Like not more than a minute ago."

He finally looked up and stared point blank at her as if she had gone completely mad. His jaw clenched and his lips pursed into a harsh line.

"Not you, too. Shit, Hallie. But I guess from that little performance you just put on I shouldn't be surprised, should I?"

"Me too, what? Corey, someone was just about to fuck my brains out. Not two minutes ago. If it wasn't *you,* I'd really like to know who it was."

"Well, aside from the obvious, um…*evidence* that you nearly had your brains fucked out, considering you've lost your goddamn mind, there was nobody here. Everyone's off on the other side of the temple being crazy over there. And would you mind putting yourself back together just a little bit? Your… ah…" He gestured vaguely at her torso. "Your stuff's all kind of on display. Makes it a little tough to get any work done."

She glanced down at herself and realized for the first time that her top was still pushed up above her breasts and her panties weren't on quite straight, still shoved aside to offer a plain view of her glistening labia. Yet Corey seemed so utterly *nonchalant* about it. He just turned back to banging on whatever it was he was holding in his hand, intent on his project. His thick forearm flexed and his knuckles whitened in a hard grip around the heavy hammer he held in his hand, banging it on the oblong shape with an unexpected level of ferocity coming from him.

She found her clothes draped over her gear where she'd left them and dressed.

"What the hell are you beating on?" she asked, padding barefoot over to him.

"This fucking…light bulb. Or whatever it is. I need to know how it works."

"It looks like a rock now," she said. "Let me see."

She reached for it. After another ineffectual bang that made his hammer bounce off he cursed and handed it to her.

"This is the weird rock Erika saved from the entrance. You think she wants you to beat on it like that?"

"It's not *just* a rock. Look at this." He took it from her and leaned over to jab it down into the glowing fire pit beside him. The pale embers inside the pit had surprised them all when they'd found it. They behaved like coal, but never disintegrated into ash, retaining their integrity after being lit multiple times with no apparent change. Erika had just brushed it off. The rest of them seemed to shrug and go on with business. If Erika was fine with it, they should be, too, right?

Hallie watched the small oblong shape as it began to glow after being plunged into the gravel of the fire pit. No ash lay inside it, only a level layer of small stones that constantly glowed and emitted heat. They'd discovered the night before that the temperature grew hotter closer to the center, and Kris had gauged his cooking by proximity to the middle of the fire pit.

The thought of Kris made her doubt her sanity after the weirdly vivid dream, if what Corey said was true. It had been so real. Jesus, her pussy was still pulsing and wet from it now. She should have changed her panties, but with Corey right there it might have been a little too conspicuous. Why she felt the need to hide from him she didn't know. He was just so willfully oblivious of everything that went on around him, but she was pretty sure it all sunk in.

No, maybe he wasn't oblivious. He was just very good at hiding his reactions.

But tonight he seemed agitated, leaning against the edge of the fire pit Kris had cooked their dinner over. Corey braced one hand on the edge and reached with the other to the stone he'd shoved tapered end first into the coals.

"See this?" he said, yanking the small stone bulb out of the fire pit. "It's glowing now. After what, thirty seconds in there? It only took a second for it to light up when we opened the door at the surface. I want to know how the fuck these things work. What powers them? What the hell are they made out of?"

"So take it with us back to a lab and look at it under a microscope. We're coming back here, you know. We just need artifacts. We don't need to prove anything while we're here. Corey..." She rested a tentative hand on his shoulder and was gratified that he didn't flinch away. "This is the find of a lifetime. Just go with it. Don't over think it yet."

CHAPTER FIVE

Hallie's palm tingled when it came into contact with the warmth of Corey's body through the threadbare fabric. Corey tensed and the cotton of his t-shirt tightened over the bunched muscles of his shoulder. It was crazy that Hallie noticed that single movement, but her entire body responded to it. The push of him against her hand was like a kinetic jolt that jarred straight through her palm to her clit. As much as her principles had steered her clear before, she was definitely attracted to him. What harm would it do, really? She just needed a good fuck, after all. Especially after that…dream she'd just had. They could move on afterward.

"Like all the other men you've moved on from?" the bitchy little voice inside her head said. It only gave her a moment's pause, rationalizing that maybe she wouldn't have to move on from him if she just gave him a chance. Except that she'd thrown caution to the wind with the last guy and look where it had gotten her—on the run and loaded with so much regret she could fill a swimming pool. Did Corey even want to be saddled with her mistakes? She doubted it. But right now she was desperate enough to test the waters.

She slid her hand over his shoulder and down his arm. His thick forearm clenched tighter and she stared, mesmerized at the play of his tight muscles beneath her palm and the heat of his skin under hers. His head turned slowly to watch the movement of her hand from the corner of his eye, like he was just waiting patiently for it to happen.

Focused on the shadows his muscles cast she was acutely aware of the change in light just behind her. The shadows darkened and a foreign yet very familiar presence pressed against her back. Hands gripped her hips and she jerked her head to look over her shoulder but saw only darkened air, the breath of a shadow. She released Corey abruptly when a hand gripped her jaw and pulled her head back. She couldn't see who held her, and Corey only stood mutely as if nothing had happened beyond her having second thoughts.

The shadow's voice reverberated in a deep whisper in her ear. *"You are mine,"* it rumbled.

She tried to stifle the whimper when he released her and disappeared again.

"You having second thoughts about molesting me?" Corey asked, turning around and staring at her.

"I'm sorry about that. I've been kinda not really myself tonight."

He raised one dark eyebrow. "You mean you don't normally beg out loud to an empty room to fuck you?"

She opened her mouth to answer, then closed it again, not quite sure what she'd say. She was still aroused and confused from the strange, ethereal intruder.

And as frank and uncensored as Corey had been in the month that they'd known each other, he'd never once come across as a lecherous asshole. It was a refreshing change from the men she was used to. Honesty deserved honesty, didn't it?

"No, Corey. I don't do that. I only do that when I'm actually being teased into oblivion. It felt so real but I can't explain it, and even if I could you probably wouldn't believe me anyway."

He settled back on the edge of the fire pit and crossed his arms, the glowing stone apparently forgotten.

"Try me. I doubt you could one-up the crazy shit I've seen tonight."

"Oh?" She glanced around, remembering what he'd said about the rest of the team. "What happened to them?"

"It's a long story. Tell me yours first."

A brush of air against her back made her shiver. The breath on her neck felt like a promise and her nipples pricked beneath her flimsy cotton tank top. *"Tell him the truth,"* the whisper said.

She released the air she'd been holding in her lungs in a soft gasp when a shadowy touch grazed across her nipple. She glanced down and only saw a darkening of air, but it definitely felt like a real hand.

"You can't see?" she asked Corey.

"See what?"

"He's here now," she said. "He…drove me mad before. And he's *still* teasing me now."

Corey's eyes followed hers down to her breasts. The voice in her ear whispered, *"You like the way he looks at you."*

All she could see was the faint shadow of a hand as it slid down, long, translucent fingers sweeping over her breast. Every little graze of finger across her nipple made her quiver. His breath was dry and hot against her neck. She couldn't resist his urgent embrace, but she didn't really want to. Having Corey's eyes on her just made it all more intense. She hesitated and sensed the touch on her body pause.

"You want him to see you undone, don't you?" The voice sounded a little incredulous. An entertained chuckle sounded in her ear. *"Well, then let's give him a show."*

"Yes!" she gasped.

"Hallie?" Corey's voice was rough and uncertain. "It's all in your head, girl. Just let it go."

She whimpered when the fingertips lingering over her breasts decided to tease and pinch at her nipples.

"N-no. Oh God, this isn't in my head."

"You have that right, lover. I'm not in your head, though I would like to be."

"Why are you doing this to me?" she asked out loud. Corey's eyes widened in confusion, but it was the shadow who responded.

"Because you want me to. Because I was meant to. Because you are mine."

The shadow behind her felt as warm and substantial as a real man, yet apparently she was the only one who could sense his presence. He was strong and insistent, his lips hot on her neck and jaw. She tilted her head to give him better access.

Corey stayed glued to his spot, watching. A sheen of sweat gleamed on his brow and upper lip and the front of his cargo shorts looked like it might rip open under the pressure of his erection. It wasn't nice of her to enjoy that part, but she did. He was the man she'd been most attracted to during their expedition, but she was smart enough to figure out that she'd never measure up to what he wanted. Watching him struggle with the urge to fuck her now, while a hollow enjoyment, still gave her some validation.

She vaguely realized how uncharitable she was being to Corey, though. He was the polar opposite of the man she'd left behind. Her ex had been polite and respectful, and a liar to the core.

Corey was brash and rude most days, but honest to a fault.

So she'd gravitated to him only to realize that he was even better behaved up close. The polite dismissals. Oh so polite. And respectful. Fuck the man for not wanting to dominate and violate her.

It had been over a year, but David's confession of love still twisted like a knife in her gut. Worse than that, his pursuit when he'd learned of her pregnancy had driven her to the ends of the earth to escape him. The child wasn't meant to be. She'd begun this Hail Mary of a trip broken hearted and desperate, denying her misdirected love for the man she'd left behind and the baby she'd lost

"You are mine," the shadow had said, but something wasn't right about the way he'd said it. She was too familiar with the tone of voice of a man who meant words just like that. The

shadow's words lacked conviction. Was this just some supernatural prank? Lies were her forte and this—man or creature or whatever he was—was a very bad liar.

But he'd struck a chord. The small lie he told was twisted up with the truth. She wanted him to touch her, that was the truth. And he believed he was meant to. She could twist the belief around to her advantage.

"Yes. I want you, but you can't own me. No man can own me, you bastard. If you want me it's on my terms, you got that? Now if you're going to fuck me in front of my friend, which I would *dearly* love for you to do, stop being a little pussy and show yourself."

Corey stared at her, incredulous. She grinned back in response. He seemed transfixed by the unfastening of Hallie's shorts through no power of her own. It felt like hot, urgent fingers trying to get her naked. This…*shadow*…wanted her, whoever he was. All she knew was that he'd teased her nearly to orgasm before and was back. Maybe this time he'd finish the job.

"I'm not going to fuck you. I just want to watch you torture him a little bit," the voice said.

"Why?" Hallie asked.

"Because you want it. I can feel how much you want it. What did he do to you?"

It probably was terrible of her to resent Corey's lack of interest, but she certainly had his attention now. Corey watched her with avid concentration. Her shadow's fingers gripped her breast with one hand and the other teased again with expert care between her exposed pussy lips, rubbing her slick clit enough to make her eyes roll back in her head.

Oh, Christ. She opened her eyes to see Corey watching, his hand pressing hard against his crotch like he could keep the monster in check with enough effort. And as much as she would love to have him involved, having the hot hands of this stranger on her felt so good.

"Nothing. That's the problem. Is that so bad?"

"Kiss him."

She didn't have an obsession, did she? Maybe so, considering her blatant lie to Erika about why she'd never made a move on Corey. She had a bad habit of falling in love with men who were emotionally inaccessible. It wasn't casual sex if you were in love, right? Corey was the first man she'd been infatuated with in that way who hadn't gravitated to her like a moth to a flame. It just made her want him more, but professional courtesy dictated she maintain a boundary between them.

Now she had to breach that boundary to prove that it didn't matter anymore.

Corey still sat on the raised edge of the fire pit, his gaze fevered as he watched her. She adjusted her clothes, feeling just a little too exposed for a simple kiss, then moved to kneel between his spread legs. His arms stayed braced on the stone ledge he sat on, and he just stared at her. God, she wanted to reach out and stroke the bulge in his shorts, but didn't dare.

He stared back at her with a mixture of hunger and conflict. In that split second he reminded her of one of her older brothers. Even before kissing him she knew how it would go, but she needed to do it anyway.

His eyes were wide and curious, his brows raised in expectation. He must have known what she was doing, but he hadn't objected yet.

"Corey," she said in a voice rough with need. "I've wanted you since we met, but you've been…reserved."

"Sorry, I…have some issues I guess," he said.

She splayed her fingers wide on his thighs and moved closer. He smelled nice, even after their sweaty day and haphazard bathing ritual. She was still dirty from the trek, too, she realized. But the aroma of the jungle on him just aroused her further. She didn't like his passivity, though. He just sat there, watching, while she moved in. She pressed her lips against his throat and flicked out her tongue across the lightly stubbled skin, drawing away the salty taste of sweat.

"He wants me to kiss you," she confessed.

"Ah, right. So I get tortured to fulfill the fantasy of an invisible man, is that it?" He let out a defeated laugh.

"I guess we both do. So kiss me."

"Kiss you, huh?" he asked in a quavering voice. "That's what *he* wants?"

"It's what I want."

"Fuck," Corey muttered and gripped the sides of her head in his hands. He pressed his lips hard against hers. Hard enough to hurt, but the second his tongue plunged into her mouth she didn't care anymore. Holy fucking Christ was he a good kisser.

When she finally pulled away, breathless and elated, the look in his eyes destroyed her mood entirely.

Hallie sighed. "You want something different, don't you?"

He looked so dejected she couldn't help but reach out to him. He leaned his head into her palm when she stroked his hair.

"Yeah. I love you, Hallie…more like…like…"

"Like a sister?"

His shoulders sagged. "Yeah. I admit I'm spun up enough to nail you right now, but I would feel incredibly dirty if I did. I'd never forgive myself."

Another hand roamed down her side from behind and she shivered from the touch. Corey seemed to notice the change and his brow furrowed.

"Is he still here? Tell me if you're okay, Hallie. I'll figure out some way to make him go away."

"I will never harm you as he seems to think I might, but if you want me to show myself you have to come to me."

"No. I like what he does. I want to go to him, Corey. I know it sounds crazy. I don't even know how to find him, but he's somewhere in here."

"I get it," Corey said. "I've been out of my mind with the need for sex since dinner with no suitable prospects in sight. No offense. Are you sure you want to do this?"

"No offense taken. And yes. Yes, I'm sure."

Corey nodded and turned back to the table where he'd left the odd stone among his other gear. He picked up one of his cameras and flicked on the power.

"What're you going to do with that?" Hallie asked, pointing at the stone.

"Giving up. I'm a tech. I'm not a scientist like you guys. I just don't buy into this dragon thing, though. Erika's like the crazy cult leader and I feel like I need to be the voice of reason since nobody else is doing it. But I'm outnumbered. Starting to think if all the *scientists* believe this BS then maybe there's something to it. Hell, if you believe it…maybe 'voice of reason' is not my true calling after all."

"You've always been that haven't you?" she asked, suddenly seeing a piece of him she'd never seen before, and liking it.

"I guess. Not that anyone ever listens to me. I'm the successful member of my family, but everyone around me still acts like morons in spite of all the advice I give them. And it's not like I just volunteer it. They fucking *ask for it* and then brush it off. Why the fuck should I bother?"

She didn't have the heart to tell him she wasn't even technically a scientist—not even a fraud of one. The resumé that had gotten her onto the expedition showed her credentials as a Ph.D. in ancient Eastern religious cults. But she figured she may as well play the part if it made Corey more comfortable.

"Why don't you believe it if there's evidence to the contrary?"

"You've heard of Jim Jones, right? Let's just say at first I believed there was something in the Kool-Aid."

"And now?"

Corey nodded at the camera and tilted it toward her so the small screen was visible.

"Pretty sure the cameras can't drink Kool-Aid," he said.

CHAPTER SIX

Kol was oblivious to the sounds coming from the other chambers when he retreated to his own, slipping beneath the door with an effort of will. He felt like a fraud, pretending to be the domineering, demanding lover. She'd seen right through him. He *could* be that way. He loved the heady rush he got when he was in control and his lover did as he asked, but it never began until she asked for it to begin with.

He believed Hallie would ask for it. She *was* the one who would see him clear of this prison once and for all, but the waiting in these last crucial moments was even more tortuous than the last five hundred years. He hid inside the huge, rigid prison of his body. The massive black dragon the council had insisted he become before the temple was locked down and they were all frozen in their assigned chambers. His true form. But the truth was, he'd long since begun to hate himself for his shape. The urge for dominance was overwhelming after living that way, even in stasis. And in spite of it, he still hadn't been able to convince *her* of his need to possess her.

The door finally opened, but he kept silent, waiting to see what she would do. Two figures slipped in. One stood within the dim light of the entrance, the second moved in from behind to stand in a dark corner.

"Did she come willingly? You didn't force her, did you?"

"Yes, Shadow. She found me and asked me to explain the ritual in detail. She is here by her own choice." Kris answered out loud, causing Hallie to jerk in surprise.

"Where is he, Kris? I can't see a goddamn thing in here." But Kris didn't answer. Kol knew it was up to him now, and up to Hallie to make a decision.

He sent his breath past her to push the door closed with a soft thud. After all these years cursing the darkness, somehow he felt too exposed even with the tiny amount of light that had come through that door.

Hallie's heartbeat seemed the loudest thing in the room. She seemed to be holding her breath. He manifested his shadow into his chosen form in front of her.

"Follow my voice," he said.

"Can't you turn on a light or light a torch or something. You said you'd show yourself to me if I came. Why can't I see you?"

She still hadn't moved from her spot.

"Hallie, you can trust me. I can see you fine. I won't let you fall. Come toward my voice."

She barked out a harsh laugh that betrayed her lack of conviction in his words. "Trust you? I know better than to trust a man who believes he can *own* me. Did you actually believe that would work? Tell me, did it work on Erika? Camille? Did those dragons convince the women they should be their slaves? I highly doubt it. I know them. They'd never give in, any more than I would."

He winced at her misunderstanding of the situation. The other women had given in, as had the men, but they hadn't known the truth beforehand, either.

"Wake me first, please. Then I will tell you everything."

"Tell me just one thing now, alright? Can I leave this temple without doing what you want me to do?"

"No. The doors above are closed. They won't open again until the ritual is complete."

"Well, okay then." She took a soft footstep toward him, then another. "As long as I'm trapped, you might as well finish what you started earlier."

The determination in her voice was unexpected. She was going to go through with it, willing or not. This wasn't how it was supposed to go. She had to want him to wake up and mark her and not just because she was trapped if she didn't.

"It's true that if you don't wake me you can't leave, but someone else will come. Another team will crack open those doors. It's inevitable. The rewards are too great for most humans to resist. Like your friends. They understand because the other dragons are…" he paused, hating what he was about to say. He released a heavy breath through his nostrils. "They're better at this part of attracting humans than I am."

"What was that?" she asked in surprise, jerking her head slightly to one side. "I saw a light somewhere behind you. Do that again!"

The breath he'd just exhaled had not come from this form, which didn't breathe so much as sense, because it *was* his breath. When he'd let out that long sigh, the breath had come from his static form in the back of the room, on the far end of the pool. He emitted another breath and watched the dark light of it illuminate his long, shiny snout and brows, and the horned crown of his head where it rested in slumber along the pair of huge foreclaws. Rather than let the breath recede into his lungs again, he let it continue, pushing the magic residue back over his sleeping body until it settled on the entire surface of his skin leaving him glowing as though in phantom moonlight.

"Is that you?" Hallie asked, awe-struck. She walked faster toward him. Too fast in the darkness.

"Wait, stop!" he called out, nearly too late to keep her stepping headlong into the pool.

"What? I can't believe you think you're worse at attracting humans. Can you see how beautiful you are? And that stunt you pulled earlier. Very forward way to seduce a woman, sneaking into her dreams like that. But you know what? It worked on me."

"I didn't...what do you mean it worked?"

"Listen, dummy, I disagree with your approach but that doesn't mean I didn't absolutely love what you were doing. I'm doing this because I *choose* to. Because I want to. Consider me an adventurous spirit. And because whatever *magic* is in the air—water—whatever—in this temple is making me the horniest I've ever been in my life. And trust me, that's saying something."

"Sweet Mother, I don't know if I'm ready for women in this century," Kol muttered.

"So, you'll adapt." He could hear the smile in her voice and relief washed over him. "Now tell me why you made me stop."

"You're about to get very wet if you don't."

She let out a throaty little laugh. "I thought that was the plan. Get me hot and bothered, then have your way with me? It's a little late for that."

Kol smiled to himself. She had a point, and she also had a wicked sense of humor. The idea that he could have a woman so self-assured that might still willingly submit to him thrilled him. And he thought he might just play along a little bit to see how she responded.

"Well," he said, lowering his voice, "You should take off your clothes before you take another step."

CHAPTER SEVEN

Hallie's heartbeat raced in spite of her cocksure attitude. Strange as it was, getting naked in the dark wasn't exactly her style. She liked having everything out in the open, knowing what to expect, and being able to trust her lovers implicitly.

But it wasn't her lover that had betrayed her, was it? David had been perfect until she'd run from him. A perfect life. A perfect lover. Rich and beautiful. But a man who insisted she follow his rules. She'd been on board for love. Until shit happened.

How, she still wasn't sure. She'd gotten pregnant in spite of taking precautions. Intolerant of mistakes, David had blamed it all on her. So she'd left.

Somewhere down the road he apparently had second thoughts. When he learned she planned to keep the baby, he came after her. She'd never seen how brutal he could be until he was.

She'd seen the signs before. But the level of illumination in a room didn't matter at all when you had blinders on.

Now here she was, standing in the dark, listening to a perfect stranger—someone not even *human*—ask her to trust him enough to take off her clothes. And like a fool, she was going to.

She squatted down and reached out a tentative hand before her, searching. The surface of the water was barely six inches in front of her, and warm. He hadn't lied about that, but he *had* lied.

"Why did you lie to me?" she asked, pulling her tank top off over her head. "If you want me to trust you so badly, tell me that."

He remained quiet, she guessed he was trying to figure out what lie he had told. Oh, God, she hoped there weren't more than the one. When he spoke, his voice seemed a little more distant than before, like he'd retreated to the far end of the room.

"I think I wanted to believe it, to believe I could make you mine simply by commanding it. I'm not as good as the others at making humans believe what I tell them."

"I believed everything else you told me. Was any of that a lie?"

"No."

She stood and shimmied out of her shorts and panties in the dark, then pulled the clip out of her hair, letting the silky waves fall to her shoulders.

"Are you going in with me?"

"I can't. Not yet, anyway. Just follow my voice."

"Did you consider just, you know...*asking*? Unless you mean you don't really want me in the first place, in which case, why bother?"

Hallie fumbled back down in the dark to grip the edge of the pool. She sat on the smooth stone and slipped her feet into the warm water. The residual ache from her journey immediately began to dissipate from her sore calves. She slipped the rest of the way into the warm depths, her feet coming to rest on the floor of the pool with the water just covering her breasts. She stood there, staring into the blackness and hoping to catch just a glimpse of him or anything that would let her know where to go. All she had so far was the hard stone at her back and the warm water surrounding her.

Her heart raced at the unknown, but so far nothing about this entire encounter had felt the least bit sinister. In spite of the utter lack of visibility, she had the strongest impression of a man trapped and lonely, and very reluctant to ask for what he really needed.

But she decided she wanted *him*, not this shadowy manifestation he'd been communicating with, and she understood from Kris's explanation that there was only one way to get to him. She took a deep breath, positioned herself in the direction she believed he rested, then threw caution to the wind.

She stretched out her arms and dove beneath the water, eyes closed and aiming forward as surely as if the pool had been lit and she could see the markers on the opposite wall. She only had the sense of the distance from the soft glow on the sleeping dragon at the far end. Her Shadow had to be there somewhere, too.

The smooth stone of the pool's wall met her fingertips and she grabbed on and stood, grateful that the pool seemed to have a uniform depth. She definitely didn't feel like treading water.

His massive, sleeping shape rested peacefully a few feet from the edge of the pool. She hoisted herself out. Her nipples immediately prickled slightly in the cooler air and gooseflesh rose on her skin.

She sat for a moment at the edge of the pool catching her breath. In spite of the stillness around her, she could feel the pulse of life from the large, static form behind her. That was *him*. She cut her eyes to the side and caught a glimpse of a massive thigh and claw. To the other side she saw a resting snout, the graceful introduction to a head the size of one of the black leather seats in David's Maserati. But prettier and still glowing faintly with the ethereal light he'd cast on its surface. God, he had *horns*. Big, coiling things that shot out from his brows.

"This is you?"

"It is."

"I just have to be in contact right?" she asked in a whisper, sure he was close enough to hear.

"Yes." The rough voice was right against her ear. "Just touch me, I'll do the rest." She could sense the warmth of his body nearby, but he still had yet to touch her again.

"I can make myself come, if you don't want to do it."

The sensation of soft fingertips grazed over her hip and down her ass. "I want you. When you wake me up, I'll want you even more."

"I want you, too," she whispered. "I just haven't decided yet whether I can trust you. Call it an overabundance of caution."

"What is it you need me to say?"

Too many different things sprang into her mind at once, but none of them had any bearing on what really worried her. She dug her fingernails into the smooth scales of the large, jade shape in front of her. A hesitant touch grazed her shoulder and she leaned into it. The warm shape of him gave slightly, like sinking into a hammock, then grew even more solid. Heavy arms wrapped around her and held her.

"Oh, God, if you even knew. I need you to tell me you'll never betray me. I'm afraid of falling in love and you never returning it. If you believe we belong together, I need assurance that you mean it. And if..." What she had on the tip of her tongue was the hardest thing to admit, but it was the reason she had run to begin with, and kept running. "If we *do* belong together, I want a family. But under no circumstances otherwise will I ever let myself get pregnant again."

"Again? You have a child already?"

"No," she whispered. "I wasn't ready when it happened before. He was a good man, but the idea of my pregnancy changed him. I betrayed his trust, but he betrayed mine. He chased me, threatened me."

Her Shadow's voice sounded gritty with anger and he held her tighter. "You didn't fight him?"

"I *trusted* him. It was his child, too. But soon I was just the vessel for the baby and his feelings for me didn't matter."

Hallie turned in the invisible arms and looked imploringly into the shadows before her, wishing she knew where his face was.

"Up here," he said. Warm fingertips touched her chin, tilting her head up higher.

"I wish I could see you," she said.

"How's this?" The air shifted slightly in front of her, and the faintest outline of a face shimmered, then disappeared, but it lingered long enough for her to see the concerned press of a pair of lovely lips and furrowed brows in a strong, open, and honest face.

"Better," she said with a small smile.

"What did you do after that?" he asked.

"The only think I could think of. I ran. I thought I'd left him behind. Then he found me. So I ran again. But he *kept coming*. Accused me of robbing him of love and family. He offered money. Insisted I come back and be a family, but I couldn't have a child with *him*. Not after what he'd turned into."

"And the child?"

"I miscarried. After that, I wanted to get as far away from it as possible. But I found Erika, and the others. And now you."

His arms shifted, one large hand caressing the small of her back. Warm lips pressed against her forehead.

"I will never betray you, I will love you forever, and if we didn't belong together, another woman would be standing here in my arms right now. Also, it's against my nature to lie to someone I love."

Something in his voice carried a hint of despair.

"You're not talking about me when you say that, are you?"

"I'm talking about you, and one other who I lost. It was a long time ago. She's gone now."

Hallie didn't miss the hint of equivocation in his voice. She pinched his naked, ethereal backside hard enough for her fingers to meet through his foggy flesh. He jerked against her.

"Ow!"

"You are a lousy liar, or at least terrible at hiding things you'd rather not say. Spill it or I'm diving back in that pool and leaving. I don't care if I end up rotting away in some dark corner. You want me, you tell me everything."

"Sweet Mother. Alright! I was in love with a human woman before I came here. I broke the rules and lost her."

"So dragons have rules, huh? Which one did you break?"

"The one that said we must mark a human if they find out our true nature. It guarantees their loyalty, among other things." The sulky tone made her wonder a few things.

"How old are you?"

"Five hundred and twenty five."

"And you've been stuck here for all but twenty five of those years. No wonder you're such a broody mess. Five hundred years and you still haven't gotten over her."

"It isn't about *her*. You don't understand, it means I have to mark *you*. They took her away because I failed to do what was expected…*required*. But I *hate* that rule."

"So you have to mark me, so what? I saw the others get marked in Corey's video. That didn't look so bad. Looked pretty damn hot, if you ask me."

"This man you were running from, did he ever give you anything…permanent?"

"Just the determination to avoid assholes who want to treat me like a vessel for their offspring."

"That's what it would signify if I do it. You would be branded like livestock. Except it would be more than that. It would tie you to me like a contract."

"Oh," she said, realizing suddenly two things. First, that his cock had just gotten epically stiffer against her stomach at the talk of marking her, and second, that his words were exactly counter to the signals his invisible body was throwing off.

"You want it, deep down. So where's the conflict?"

His forehead rested on her shoulder and he groaned. "I don't believe in treating humans like …breeding stock. But yes, it's instinctual. I have to fight the urge."

Was she crazy that the idea turned her on incredibly?

"Come here," she said. She backed up, pulling him with her until the wall of the stone dragon behind her hit the flesh of her ass. She reached up and tangled her fingers into the short hair at the back of his neck, pulling him into a kiss. He sank against her, as hard and solid as flesh now, his tongue delving deeper at her invitation. He tasted faintly of juniper and something a little salty. Would he have the same flavor in his true form? Oh, God, did she want to find out how he tasted—every inch of him.

"Sweet Mother, women are confusing now," he said when she came up for breath.

"How in the world do you have short hair after five hundred years?" She raked her fingernails along his scalp when he bent to her breast, sucking deftly on one nipple, flicking it delicately with his tongue and pulling at it with his lips.

"Dragon magic," he whispered, brushing lips against her other nipple and pushing one hand down between her thighs. "You're even wetter than you were before. How are you so wet?"

"Dragon magic," she said with a gasp when he thrust a pair of fingers deep inside. "What else can you do with it besides make me beg you to fuck me? Oh, God, whatever you're doing, do it harder."

He laughed against her nipple. "Give it to me, love, so I can have you for real. Give me your Nirvana."

He relentlessly fucked her with both fingers. He found her sweet spot and now rubbed at it while he thumbed her clit. She reached for his cock, the beautiful thick length that she'd wished for when he woke her up earlier. She wanted him to fuck her now, but knew this little taste was just an appetizer. Soon she'd have the genuine article, not a facsimile.

The mountain of dragon flesh behind her began to quiver when her orgasm began. The pleasure rocketed through her so hard she wasn't sure if it was the earth moving under her feet or if she'd merely lost balance from the effect of him. Soon it became clear he was no longer holding her up from the front, his fingers were no longer sunk deep in her pussy, but something altogether bigger had gripped her from behind, then lifted her, cradling her gently in a pair of massive talons.

A massive, shiny black head peered down at her, tilted to one side. As her spasms subsided, she abstractly thought that if David ever found her again, he might be in danger of being eaten.

"That's it, Hallie," her dragon's deep voice reverberated off the walls in the room. "I'm going to fuck you so hard we wake the entire temple without the Queen's help. But first, please tell me you want my mark. Tell me you'll have me."

The desperation in his tone contradicted the majestic ebony beast that held her. In that moment she understood it wouldn't be she who was bound to him, but the other way around. He would be in thrall to her. She was as sure of it as she was that she would never have to run from him.

"Do it now, but first tell me who you are. I need to know the *name* of the dragon I'm essentially marrying."

CHAPTER EIGHT

She said yes!" Kol vibrated with the excitement of her answer, unable to resist sending the thought out to all the others who could hear. Now he would be able to have her without betraying his brethren, forcing them into another long sleep.

"I heard her, Shadow," Kris sent the thought from somewhere in the darkness at the other end of the room. *"Don't leave me hanging, finish the final step. It's MY turn next."*

"Let me savor this moment. I know you're eager, but trust me, I think we'll both want time to recover so we can enjoy being a part of the Nexus. As will the others. And you can't begin without all of us."

"Kol," he said, regaining his senses and gazing down at the beautiful woman in his arms. "My name is Kol. This may sting a bit."

Hallie arched her back, thrusting her breasts up to him. Kol nuzzled them with his long snout and she laughed. "That tickles."

"Sorry, I'm not used to staying in this form for very long. The world has always been a little too small for me."

With a long, forked black tongue, he traced the pattern of the mark between her breasts: a medallion-shaped crest with a coiled dragon within—black to represent his color. She hissed in response to the sting and he quickly exhaled a steamy breath to soothe her skin. The magic of their bond wasn't instant, but within the span of a heartbeat his craving for possession dissipated, replaced only with the need to pleasure her.

Unable to resist the allure of her twin, pink-tipped mounds he darted his tongue out to taste her.

She sighed and arched further, grabbing onto him and pressing her mouth against the side of his, her breast closer to his tongue.

"Go lower," she whispered.

He complied, flicking his tongue along the smooth skin of her stomach. Her hips twitched and she spread her legs for him when he reached the fringed mound of her sex. Slowly and delicately he parted her slick lips with the forked tip of his tongue. She tasted of earth and rain and sky. He delved deeper, tasting, teasing, enjoying how her juices flowed over his tongue the deeper he went.

A low, contented purr rose up through his chest. She was his now, and her surrender to him tasted even sweeter than the creamy dew between her thighs. Her orgasm took her more slowly that time, washing through her over several seconds and leaving her limp and languid in his talons. Kol relished the clench of her muscles around his tongue, letting it linger inside her a moment before withdrawing and licking his lips.

She winced and shifted within his loose clutch.

"I can change if this is uncomfortable for you," he rumbled.

"Don't you dare. Now that I've had a taste of what dragon magic is good for, you're showing me all the tricks."

"I've never made love to a woman like this. I think I would hurt you."

"What good is such a beautiful shape if you don't use it? I'm sure we can improvise."

Kol blinked at her. He couldn't possibly…he glanced down at the massive ebony erection between his scaled thighs, easily the size of one of his arms in his human shape. He remembered how tight she had been around his fingers and tongue. It didn't matter how juicy her sweet pussy was, there was no way he'd fit. Sweet Mother, he wanted to be inside her, but to abuse her perfect pussy that way was unthinkable. There had to be a way to please her without hurting her.

"As you wish," he said finally. "But we're going slow and we're doing it my way."

Eveline had asked him for one thing at the end, and he had failed her. He wouldn't let Hallie be disappointed.

He shifted into his human form, leaving only his wings still manifested, twin extensions of his wide shoulders. He carried her to the pool, then stepped off the edge, still holding her cradled in his arms. Before his feet could hit the water, he extended both wings and hovered, lowering them slowly into the warm, dark pool until his feet rested on the bottom. He let his wings fade back into his shoulder blades.

"Stretch out," he whispered when Hallie's body broke the surface of the water. "I'll support your weight."

Hallie obeyed, stretching out across the surface with her arms above her head.

"That's it. Arms out. Feel the warmth. Let it sink into you. You swam too quickly to find me earlier, the soak would have done you good."

"Let me guess, dragon magic has healing properties?" she asked

"Among other things, yes."

Kol kept one hand beneath the center of her back, then moved the other over her. She tensed when the additional support disappeared. He quickly bent his head and kissed her, a long, languid press of lips sliding across lips, tongue thrusting between until she relaxed again.

"Stay with me," he said.

"It feels like I'm weightless," she said. "But I can feel your heat. And your cock keeps rubbing against my hip."

"I know," he growled. "I'll have it inside you soon enough. Can you feel this?"

He caressed the underside of her breast, tracing fingertips around and around until they converged on her nipple. She sighed, growing even more pliant under his touch. The scent of her arousal grew stronger with each caress and he inhaled. Eveline had smelled like this and he had always loved drawing the aroma out of her along with the sweet sounds she made. He gave Hallie's nipple a light pinch and enjoyed her sharp intake of breath and the way her chest began to rise and fall more quickly.

He shifted his hand to the other breast, repeating the action while he bent to wrap his lips around the first. The skin of her areola puckered against his tongue.

"Yes," she whispered. "Oh yes."

"Shh. Quiet now. Just let yourself feel me."

She nodded slightly and her mouth opened with a soft little gasp when his fingertips trailed lower, past her navel, and slipped between her pussy lips. Her bud pulsed under his touch, already swollen and ready again, but it would have to wait. He slipped two fingers between her lips and sank them into her, deeper than before. The magic that infused the water provided lubrication to supplement her own fluids. Her hips raised up to meet each slow thrust of his fingers and her slick muscles tightened around them.

Kol continued sucking and teasing her breasts with his mouth and gradually added another finger to her wet depths. Then another. Soon he had four fingers in.

"Tell me if you want me to stop."

She shook her head. "No. I want to feel you. All of you."

His cock throbbed hot against the soft swell of her backside. She could take him as he was in his human form, but not his true size. His siblings had always experimented with their sizes, the twins in constant competition with who could manifest bigger than the other. Preferring his human form he'd never quite mastered the middle-ranges. It was either his human form, or his dragon form, no in between.

He had an idea of how to find a suitable middle ground with Hallie. With her marked now, he hoped it would work.

"I'm going to add another now. Promise me you'll tell me if I'm hurting you."

"How...how many?" she panted.

He swallowed hard as he gently pressed, adding his thumb to the tight, wet sheathe of her. Beads of sweat trickled down his temples. Her pussy clamped like a vise around his hand.

"Relax. Take a deep breath and relax. Hallie, I don't want to hurt you."

"You're not h-hurting. Oh, God, Kol. That feels too good."

When she relaxed again, he pushed a little deeper and murmured in her ear, "What feels good? This?" He twisted his hand so that the knuckle of his thumb rubbed against her sweet spot, then slowly began to close his fingers into a fist. She bucked violently, splashing water and gripping his arm tightly with one hand.

"Oh God, yes!"

His closed fist pushed, rubbed, and pushed incrementally deeper. Soon, he'd reached her limit and pulled back out. The walls of her pussy clenched and released around him. Hallie's head fell back and she moaned incoherently when he pushed his hand back into her to the wrist.

He found it hard to draw breath now, watching her come undone under his careful attention. Her pussy clenched around his hand, but she took it without complaint. On the contrary, she had grown even wetter.

It seemed that not a drop of blood was left in his head to keep him sane—it had all rushed to his pulsing groin, his thick shaft eager to be inside that hot, velvet chamber and feel her milk him until he came.

Hallie cried out, low and rough. He kissed her and held tight with his free hand while she came.

He carefully pulled his hand out of her and spun her on the surface the water so that her legs were on either side of his hips. "I think you're ready. Promise me you will speak if anything hurts."

She gave him a feverish, low-lidded look and nodded. The flush of her glowed in the darkness, but she seemed to see him, too, and stared in rapt appreciation.

"You know you glow in the dark a little bit?" she said. "Can I see more of you?"

"It's just my sweat and breath. I can make them do things. Like this." He tilted his head back and exhaled deeply. The breath luminesced in a cloud above them both, before settling over his skin, leaving a sheen that she could see.

She surged up in the water, wrapped her legs tightly around his waist and gripped his shoulders.

"You're beautiful," she said and pressed her lips hungrily against his.

He gripped her hips, guiding her pussy down over his stiff and, for the moment, still human-sized cock. He could have come from the single stroke, as long as it had been since the last time, but knew he had to make this last, for her. They'd have other chances for other fun afterward. A lifetime of other chances.

"Oh, baby, that's it. Now get bigger. Show me that beautiful dragon again," she said.

He took a deep breath, gathering the magic into him. The process of shifting was gradual, the transformation occurring over several seconds. His cock grew along with the rest of him, pressing tighter and tighter against the walls of her pussy. At the same time, he began fucking her, surging up into her slick, inviting channel.

As he grew, she took him. Every thick, swelling inch of him thrust into her. He was too lost in ecstasy to realize that he'd done it. He'd fully shifted and she hadn't said to stop. Now, she was moaning and writhing hard against him, her legs splayed wide across his scaled hips, working herself on him. Her pussy muscles clenched and released while she gripped his shoulders, riding him and meeting the surging rhythm of his thrusts.

He clutched her hips in his taloned claws and bent his head to sweep the forked tip of his tongue around her nipples, both at once. With slow, careful effort, he lifted her up his length, then let her sink back down. The tight, wet friction sent tremors of pleasure through him, all the way to the tip of his tail.

Haunches braced beneath him, he leaned forward, laying her down along the surface of the water. She gazed up at him, face constricted in desperate tension, but she relaxed and let her arms fall back to float in the water above her head. With one gentle talon, he lifted each of her legs, pulling them up to rest her ankles against his wide, black-scaled chest.

"Give me your Nirvana again, Hallie. I want to feel it surge into me when I give you mine."

"Y-you can feel it?" she asked breathily.

He resumed the slow, push-pull of his hips against hers and looked down to where they were joined. Her pussy was stretched impossibly around the thick, black girth of his shaft. Her pretty little clit throbbed bright pink in contrast. He dipped his snout and snaked out his tongue to tease at the tiny bundle. Her tangy juices tingled on his tongue. He licked again and she arched her back. The tighter clench of her pussy muscles and the sudden slackness of her legs spreading just a little wider signaled she was close.

"Give it to me *now*," he growled, swirling his tongue around her clit and slamming hard into her. The hot friction drove him wild. He couldn't hold back a second longer, but it seemed neither could she.

She yelled and thrashed in the water. He held her torso to keep her head above the surface. Wet ripples flowed over her breasts and stomach, lapping at her skin with the undulations of her body while she came. Her pussy pulled relentlessly at his cock, urging the hot stream of cum that flowed into her. A loud roar escaped his throat as he came and his balls constricted, sending every last drop into her willing depths.

She fell limp in his grasp, gasping for breath when it was over. Worried, he quickly shifted back to his preferred shape and lifted her, sliding his half-hard cock out of her. He extended his wings and lifted them both out of the water, landing at the edge of the pool.

Stooping, he began to lay her down, but the hard floor of his chamber wouldn't do for her. With the power of a thought and a heavy exhale, a large, black bed formed in the spot where he'd lain asleep for five hundred years waiting for her to find him. He laid her gently on its soft surface, then climbed on behind her and tucked her into his arms.

"Women in this century are surprising, and wonderful," he said, caressing her temple with his lips.

"No," Hallie murmured. "Just this woman, and you'd better not forget it."

CHAPTER NINE

Hallie woke a little later to the sensation of a warm, flesh-and-blood body beneath her cheek. She opened her eyes and glanced around in surprise. The chamber was awash in a warm glow from sconces like the others in the temple.

She looked at Kol's sleeping face for the first time without the shade of darkness or invisibility between them. His fine features were startling. She didn't usually go for pretty boys, preferring… well, large and *swarthy*, if she had to put a name to it. But she decided he was a far cry from unappealing, and he did have the *large* part down, even when he wasn't in his dragon form.

His black eyebrows, twitched in his sleep, perhaps from a dream of her. His skin was very fair, almost translucent, but his hair was jet black and, at the moment, sticking out in every direction.

Full, pink lips parted when she grazed her fingertips over them. This was the mouth that had started it all—its wide bow shape was very kissable. She traced fingertips over the line of his jaw, down over his neck and shoulder, across hairless, angular planes of chest and abs. Strange, she'd had the sense of a kind of velveteen texture over his scales when he was in his dragon form and she could feel the same thing now, but couldn't see it.

Whatever it was, it tingled like soft down against her palm when she moved her hand lower. She paused at the swath of black fabric covering the rising erection that rested in a long, thick shape beneath his navel.

Hallie gently tugged the sheet off, baring him to her entirely from head to hips.

God, he was as magnificent like this as he was shifted. His cock twitched under her light touch, fully awake and aroused even while Kol still slept. The sight of him caused a pleasant, aching heat to grow between her thighs. Experimentally, she clenched her vaginal muscles tight, testing for pain, but there was nothing aside from a comfortable soreness.

She raised up slowly and quietly, straddled his hips, and lowered herself down the thick length of him, enjoying the pleasant friction of that first stroke.

With the third stroke he finally roused enough to push back, though it may have just been a reflex. His brow creased in confusion and his hands slid up to her thighs.

"Hmm, you just take what pleases you, don't you?" he murmured, finally opening his eyes.

"I have this little mark that says I can, at least from you," she said.

"You could never take from me, Hallie. All I am, I give you freely." He shoved his cock harder into her for emphasis, then sat up, wrapping his arms around her.

Eyes as dark as night gazed into hers while she took him in. Did he even have pupils? She leaned closer and saw that yes, there was the barest hint of variegation in his iris, but it nearly disappeared when his pupils widened in response to the clench of her pussy around him.

His hands slid down her back to grip her ass and she shifted to wrap her legs around his hips. In movements that mimicked his water-borne fucking before they slept, he tilted her, laying her flat on the bed. The angle let him sink deeper and she sighed in pleasure at the way even his human cock could reach all the best parts of her just fine. But she was an adventurous spirit, she had to know how it felt to fuck a dragon.

This time she came only with the deep strokes of his cock rubbing against her slick walls and the whispers of endearment in her ear. Dirty endearments, like, "I loved the way your sweet pussy tasted when you came on my tongue. I love the taste of your Nirvana when you give it to me. It tastes like power. It feeds me."

The pulse of his orgasm, hot inside her sent her beyond the edge and farther.

Her sensibilities kicked in when the pleasure subsided and she pulled away abruptly, that cold, "Oh shit" feeling sinking into her. She'd let him come inside her. Could dragons and humans even crossbreed? She shifted and sat at the edge of the bed, dipped her fingers between her thighs and brought back cream-covered fingertips. The heady scent of the two of their juices mixed made her a little dizzy and undeniable lust welled up in her again, but she'd already been a fool once. This she needed to know, and now. *More like yesterday*, she thought, but she'd been too overcome with the powerful pull of lust to think straight.

"Kol," she said in a quavering voice.

"What is it?" he said, immediately by her side with a comforting hand at her back.

"Can...you get me pregnant?"

She stared straight at him, watched concern mix with confusion and a kind of pleased curiosity. "If you want me to, I will, but it isn't possible in the temple."

She shook her head, confused. "No, I mean *dragons and humans*. Can we...you know...have babies. Christ, I can't believe I was so stupid not to even *ask* before. I brought condoms but nobody's done any screwing during this trip besides Erika and Eben. I haven't been on the pill in months."

His brows drew together. "You don't want to get pregnant?"

"Will you just answer the goddamn question?"

"Yes! That's what we do. It's the whole point of the ritual, to find suitable mates for the purpose of, well, *mating*. But..." His face relaxed and he lowered his head and sighed. "This is about the man who chased you. The baby you weren't prepared to have ...or to lose."

Hallie couldn't respond, her throat already too knotted up with frustration and incomprehension.

"Hallie, there is no such thing as an unwanted, unexpected dragon child. We breed when we are ready." He touched the black emblem etched above her heart. "Your mark ensures that even if I wanted it, if you weren't ready, it wouldn't happen. And even if we *both* wanted it right now, it isn't possible for a dragon child to be conceived within the temple. It prevents inbreeding in the last days before we sleep."

"Why us, though?"

Kol sighed. "It's a long story. Centuries long, really. We used to be hunted, feared. Our numbers dwindled so we had to take steps to ensure our race survived. Hence the ritual. But those of us that remained were too close by blood. Humans are the only race on Earth worthy of mating with."

Hallie stood and walked away, needing a second to process the information. She slipped back into the warmth of the pool and dipped her head under water.

She could have everything with him. More than that, she could have her life back. And a child someday, too. His child, but only if she was ready. Lungs hungry for air, she breached the surface again and inhaled.

Kol crouched at the edge watching. "It's a lot to digest in a few hours, I know, but this is only the beginning, Hallie. It is my only dream in life to make you happy. And only you."

He slipped into the water and pulled her into his arms.

"Good," she said and let him kiss her.

While they embraced, a slew of excited, chattering voices washed into the room and they turned. The entire crowd of their friends traipsed in through the doors and began diving into the other end of the pool.

"What the hell?" Hallie said, irritated at their interruption.

Camille swam up to them, eyes wide and mouth open in an excited smile. "Wow, Hallie. He's pretty. Not as pretty as Roka, but he looks right for you."

"What are you guys doing?" Hallie asked.

"Roka said the best place to bathe was in here, and since the phase was over and the doors unlocked, we just came right in.

Gotta get ready for Kris's big performance. He's so, so excited. We just wanted to wash a bit of grime off first. It's gonna get very, *very* dirty in there. I can't wait!"

Kol chuckled when Camille swam away and was promptly lifted up and kissed soundly by a large, white-haired man who Hallie assumed must be the one called Roka. Roka passed her into Eben's arms, who then diligently and carefully began rinsing her from head to toe. After a moment it looked less like washing and more like fondling.

"Don't be mad," Kol said. "They're excited. The next phase will be a sight to see, and we all have to be there."

A throat cleared from the edge of the pool and Hallie looked up. Corey gave her a tentative wave. "Hey," he said with a sideways smile, then his brow quickly furrowed in concern. "You alright? I admit I heard…sounds that worried me." His eyes shifted uncertainly to Kol.

Her face relaxed, pleased that he'd thought to ask. "Yes, I'm better than alright. Corey, this is Kol."

Corey reached down and shook Kol's hand amiably.

"I've decided to take him home with me after we're done here," she added.

Corey's eyebrows raised. "Oh? I didn't think you had a home, being on the run and all."

Hallie blinked and stared at him, open-mouthed.

He grinned. "You think we didn't all know from the beginning? Erika still insisted you were right for the team even though you were outright lying to us. That woman has the strangest instincts, but I've known her a long time and learned not to second-guess her."

"Even about all this stupid *dragon stuff*?" Hallie asked pointedly.

He shrugged. "I'm still on the fence about it. Too much indiscriminate sex, as far as I'm concerned. And I'm still not sure where the hell I fit in considering all of you have paired up."

"There are only two dragons unaccounted for," Kol interjected. "Issa just left with Kris, and I don't see her mark on anyone. She's probably preparing him for the next phase."

"Who's the other one?" Hallie asked.

Kol stared at them both like they were imbeciles. "The other one is the Queen."

ABOUT OPHELIA BELL

Ophelia Bell loves a good bad-boy and especially strong women in her stories. Women who aren't apologetic about enjoying sex and bad boys who don't mind being with a woman who's in charge, at least on the surface, because pretty much anything goes in the bedroom.

Ophelia grew up on a rural farm in North Carolina and now lives in Los Angeles with her own tattooed bad-boy husband and four attention-whoring cats.

You can contact her at any of the following locations:
Website: http://opheliabell.com/
Facebook: https://www.facebook.com/OpheliaDragons
Twitter: @OpheliaDragons
Goodreads: https://www.goodreads.com/OpheliaBell

Printed in Great Britain
by Amazon